TOGETHER FOREVER

by
Roderick Cox and Tobias Lagemann

Cornelsen

Together Forever
Roderick Cox, Tobias Lagemann

Verlagsredaktion
Susanne Döpper

Umschlaggestaltung
Heike Börner, dia

Titelbilder
G&M David de Lossay / Image Bank, Berlin
Corel Library

Illustration
Roy Schofield, Cheam
Gabriele Heinisch, Berlin

Technische Umsetzung
Peter Richter

Für die freundliche Unterstützung bedanken wir uns bei:
Andrew Davies, Heerlen (NL); Frank Donoghue, Nenagh, Tipperary (IRL); Birgit Herrmann, Aachen

www.cornelsen.de

1. Auflage, 4. Druck 2009

Alle Drucke dieser Auflage sind inhaltlich unverändert und können im Unterricht nebeneinander verwendet werden.

Druck: CS-Druck CornelsenStürtz, Berlin

ISBN 978-3-464-37162-6

Inhalt gedruckt auf säurefreiem Papier aus nachhaltiger Forstwirtschaft.

CONTENTS

CHAPTER ONE

"Hallo, everybody, on this hot, hot day. It's three o'clock and it's very sunny. And it's going to stay like this. Just right for the weekend. And what's on Radio Chester this afternoon? It's our drugs special, with lots and lots of information about drugs and how to stay away from them. Because you all know, drugs can kill. Here's a song about this, *Julie's in the drug squad,* from our old friends, The Clash."

It wasn't very busy at *Stringers Restaurant* on this Friday afternoon. It really was terribly hot. Nobody wanted to eat hamburgers. But on the other side of the road, outside *McFarlane's Ice-Cream,* there were long queues of students from Brookland School. They all wanted to eat a cool ice-cream – and not a hot hamburger! Claire Hall knew how they felt. But she had to wait another two hours till she finished work. And when she had finished work, her weekend – and her holiday – could start. Claire was very excited.

"Hi, Claire!" Somebody tapped her on the shoulder.
Claire turned around.
"It's me, Andy, Andrew Wilson. Remember?"
"Yes, of course. Sorry. You surprised me," Claire said. "I was thinking about things."
Andy was an old friend from long ago.
"What were you thinking about?" asked Andy.
"My holiday," said Claire.

"Are you going on holiday?" asked Andy.

"I told you last month."

"I remember now. You said you were going to France."

Claire laughed. "Oh, Andy, not France. I'm going to Germany. I want to visit my father. He lives in Cologne."

"Now, young man, what would you like to eat?" It was Mr Stringer, the owner of the restaurant.

"Hamburger and chips, please," said Andrew.

Claire went a little red. Mr Stringer paid *her* to ask the customers what they wanted to eat.

"Can I buy you a cola?" Andrew asked Claire.

"No, thank you. I have to work," Claire said. "Maybe when I've finished."

"It's OK, Claire," said Mr Stringer. "It's your last day today. You can finish now. And we aren't exactly the busiest place in town this afternoon." Mr Stringer looked sadly across the street to *McFarlane's Ice-Cream*.

"Thank you, Mr Stringer," said Claire and smiled. She sat down with Andy at a table near the window.

"That was a great match," Andy said.

"Yes, it was," Claire said. She had seen Andy at the big match, Manchester City against Manchester United.

"Here you are, young man, your hamburger and chips," said Mr Stringer. "And your cola, Claire."

"Thank you, Mr Stringer," said Claire.

"Do you still have your motor bike?" asked Andrew.

"Of course!" said Claire and smiled. After the match she had really enjoyed showing Andrew her motor bike. It wasn't a new bike, but it was her first bike. And that's always something special. Her Uncle Harry had lent her the money for it and she had had to promise to work in the school holidays.

"If you want something, you have to work for it," Uncle Harry had said.

"Are you going to France on your motor bike?"

"Andy, I'm not going to France, I'm going to Germany. I'm going to visit my father. I've just told you that."

"Yes, I'm sorry, Claire."

"Are you OK?" asked Claire.

Her old friend really didn't look good. He was pale and his hands were shaking.

"I'm OK," said Andy. "I just have to go to the toilet – now!"

Claire watched him walk away from the table. He was so thin.

The two young people sat for an hour in *Stringers*. Andrew Wilson ordered some more chips.

"I just love chips," he said and laughed.

They talked a lot about Claire's trip to Germany.

"It must be fun to travel so far on a motor bike," said Andrew.

"Yes, I'm really excited," said Claire.

"How are you travelling to Germany? Via Hull or via Dover? If you go via Hull, your journey in England isn't so long, but it's a 14-hour crossing from Hull to Rotterdam. But from Rotterdam it isn't too far to Cologne."

"You know a lot about ferries." Claire was surprised *how* much he knew.

"You told me all about them at the match," Andy said.

"Did I?" asked Claire.

"Well? Which way are you going to Germany?"

"Via Dover, of course. I don't want to spend hours on a ferry. I want to ride my motor bike. And I'm going the old-fashioned way, by ferry, not through the boring Channel Tunnel. I'm leaving at 6 o'clock tomorrow morning."

"So you're going via Dover. Are you …?"

"Look, Andy," Claire said. "You've been here for more than an hour and we've only talked about my trip. What about you? How are you? Did you get the new job you were telling me about at the match?"

"Yes, I got the job."

"And what do you do? You didn't want to tell me last month."

"Oh, nothing special. I'm a courier."

"At one of those firms like USP? Or NTT?"

"Well, it's something like that. But it's a little different."

Before Claire could ask more questions about the strange courier's job, Andrew got up.

"I'm sure we'll meet again soon," he said and paid for his food and Claire's cola. Before she could say thank you, he had walked out of the restaurant.

"He's a strange young man," Mr Stringer said, when Claire got her things from the office behind the restaurant.

"Yes, he is," was all Claire could answer. All the time he had only wanted to talk about her trip. Well, it *was* an exciting trip.

Through England from north to south, then across the Channel by ferry, and then all the way to Germany – on her motor bike! It was going to take all day.
"Say hallo to your father for me, please," said Mr Stringer as Claire left the restaurant. "When's he going to come back and visit his home town again? He hasn't been to Chester for a long time."
"Next year perhaps," said Claire. "He has to work so much, he never has time for a holiday."
"Yes, Charlie always worked a lot," said Mr Stringer.
"Goodbye, Mr Stringer. I'll see you after my holiday."
"Goodbye, Claire."

Claire got on her motor bike. She called it "Susie", a good name for a Suzuki 250. She put on her helmet and zipped up her leather jacket. Then she rode home. "Susie" felt fantastic today.

As she turned into Elm Road, Mr Hitchcock waved to her. The old man spent all day in his garden. Sometimes he just sat in a chair, at other times – very often really – he mowed the lawn. And every Sunday he worked on his roses. Claire was surprised that the flowers hadn't died yet.

"Mum!" Claire shouted as she walked into the house. She could smell food. Claire thought it was chilli con carne. What was her mother thinking of? On this hot day a fruit salad was much better.
"Mum!" she shouted again.
Nobody answered. The house was empty. Claire opened the kitchen door.
"Surprise, surprise!" Sharon and Dave were in the kitchen and

Asif and his girlfriend Nasreen too. Evan was there, and her new friends from the motor bike club Kevin and Georgina. And of course her brother Tom. There was a poster on the kitchen wall. "HAVE A GOOD TRIP!" it said. Claire's mother was standing behind all the young people.
"I don't know what to say," said Claire. "What a fantastic surprise! I just don't know what to say."
Everybody laughed. "Let's go into the garden," said Mrs Hall.

They all helped to carry the food into the garden. Then they sat down at the garden table in the shade of the big tree that Claire had watched growing outside her bedroom window over the last seven years. In spite of the terribly hot weather, they were having Claire's favourite meal, chilli con carne. On the barbecue were Claire's other favourites, jacket potatoes and sausages.

There was lots and lots of talking in the Halls' garden on this super summer Friday evening. They talked about Claire's trip to Germany, of course. But the young people talked about their plans for the future too. Claire was going to continue her education at Chester Sixth Form College. Dave was going to go to Midland College in Birmingham. He wanted to be a car mechanic. His girlfriend Sharon was going to start a secretarial course at Chester College. And Asif and Evan were starting at the police college in Manchester.
"Will you have enough time for your running, Asif?" asked Georgina.
"Sport is very important for police officers," Asif explained.
"But I'm sure you have to learn so much if you want to be a police officer. All those rules and laws."
Asif laughed. "You all know I can learn faster than I can run."

"And you can run very, very fast," said Kevin.
Asif was the best 800 metre runner in Chester. He was usually in the first five at the junior national championships. His coaches were sure that their "boy" was going to win an Olympic medal one day. Asif wasn't so sure. That's why he was starting his training at the police college.
"When I'm older and can't run, I'll have a job," he had told his friends when they were all still at school.

It was a long evening. When Claire went to bed, it was almost 11 pm. But her panniers were already packed. She was glad that she had listened to her mother and had packed her things for the journey two days earlier.

When Claire got up at 5.15 the next morning, she was still very happy.
"I'm leaving soon," she thought.

Her mother was already waiting in the kitchen.
"Oh, Claire, my little girl, time goes so quickly."
Claire looked at the kitchen clock.
"It's OK, Mum. I have another thirty minutes."
"No, no, I don't mean that."
"I know, Mum."
"You're so grown-up," said Mrs Hall.
Claire laughed. "Oh, Mum. I'm not really grown-up."
Mrs Hall took Claire in her arms.
"My little girl, my little Claire."

At 6 o'clock Claire started her motor bike. As she rode out of Elm Road and turned into Woodlake Road, Mr Hitchcock waved to her. Claire was surprised that her neighbour was in his garden so early. She had never seen him at this time before. She made the motor bike roar goodbye to Mr Hitchcock. In her mirror she could see that he was still waving. The old neighbour had got up early just for her. She had tears in her eyes.
"Silly wind!" she thought, as she rode away from her home.

The first part of her long journey was through Chester's city centre. There wasn't much happening at 6 o'clock in the morning. All the shops were still closed. Two young men were waiting for a bus. They looked very tired. Claire wondered if they had got up early or if they hadn't been to bed yet after a long night in one of Chester's clubs.
"Goodbye, Chester," said Claire.

Five minutes later Chester was behind her. The A51 road towards the M6 motorway was empty. But near the bridge over the Shropshire Union Canal Claire saw a big motor bike next to the road. For a terrible moment she thought there had been an accident. But then she realised that the machine was still standing. It wasn't lying on the ground.

Claire rode onto the M6 motorway. "South: Birmingham, London" the sign said. All the way to Birmingham she thought about the big motor bike on the A51. Perhaps the rider had felt ill. Perhaps he had got off his bike and collapsed next to the road. How terrible!
But then near Birmingham the traffic got really bad. And Claire forgot the strange motor bike.

CHAPTER TWO

Claire sang an old song – "Born to be wild" – as she roared south-east along the M6 motorway. She was happy. She was going on holiday. On her own motor bike. She had worked hard for it these last two months. Six days a week, eight hours a day, with a two-hour break in the afternoon. It was harder than at school. She remembered that Uncle Harry had said that it was going to be just like that. "Claire," he had said, "you often complain about school, but you'll see that going to work is hard too."
In the two months at *Stringers Restaurant* there really had been days when she wanted to be back at school. There had even been days when Mrs Winch's PE lessons seemed better than the dirty dishes in Mr Stringer's kitchen. At times like that she had always thought about what she was working for. And suddenly everything was very easy.

And now she was on her way. She was going to Germany on her own motor bike. And she had earned the money for the holiday herself! Claire had always loved travelling. As she came past the motorway sign for Alton Towers, she remembered the roller coaster, the ghost train and the fantastic big wheel there. Yes, Claire had always liked wheels.
Then she thought about all the other trips she had had with her parents. Before her parents had divorced, the Hall family had travelled to different places every weekend in the summer. They had often been walking in the Welsh mountains and swimming at the Welsh seaside. When Claire had first seen Snowdon, the highest mountain in Wales, she had only been

five years old. The mountain had seemed enormous to her. She had travelled to Snowdon again on her first motor bike trip. The mountain was still enormous.

As Claire went past Birmingham on the M6 motorway, she thought of *Cadbury World*, the exhibition about chocolate at the famous chocolate factory in Birmingham. Claire had been seven years old when her father had said, "Would you like to see how they make chocolate, Claire?" What child could say "no" to a question like that? Claire's mother always liked to tell the story that Claire had had toothache for a week after the trip to *Cadbury World*.

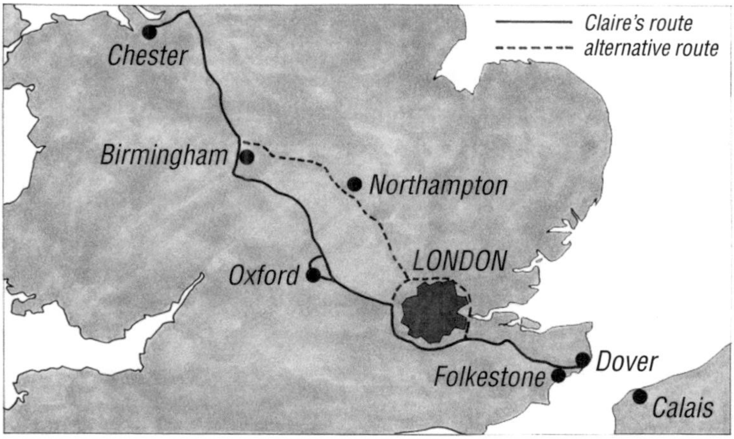

Claire had planned her route carefully. There were two good routes from Birmingham to London, via Northampton or via Oxford. Claire wanted to have a break and something to eat in Oxford, one of her favourite English cities, so she turned off the M6 after Birmingham and onto the M42 and then onto the M40. At Bicester she left the motorway and turned onto the A34 to Oxford. Claire knew that it was a detour into Oxford,

but Uncle Harry had told her, "Motorways can make you very tired. They're fast, but very boring. You need a good break. And don't go to one of those motorway cafés, where you'll just sit and think about motorways!"
Uncle Harry knew all about motor bikes and motorways. He had learned to ride a motor bike when he was in the army in Germany. He loved to tell Claire about the German *Autobahnen* and his "friends", the *Autobahnpolizei*!

Claire parked her motor bike in Oxford city centre and had a sandwich in a little café with a nice view of the river. What was its name? There were two rivers in Oxford. Was this the River Thames? Ten years ago her father had taken her to see this university town with its colleges that were hundreds of years old. While she checked her motor bike before she left town, she remembered that he had told her that students in Oxford liked to call their big rival Cambridge "The Other Place". Claire had to get to another place now – to Dover for the 13.15 ferry to Calais.

She got back on the M40 motorway towards London and 20 miles outside the city centre she turned onto the M25, the motorway ring around London, the world's longest ring road. There was lots of traffic, but it was still faster than going through the centre of London. And Claire didn't feel safe enough on her motor bike to find her way through the city of 7 million people – without having an accident with one of them. Claire remembered that Londoners often crossed the road where *they* wanted to!
After an hour on the M25 Claire turned onto the M20. "Channel Tunnel, Dover," the sign said. Just before Folkestone she went past the enormous Channel Tunnel

station, where cars were waiting to drive onto the special trains that went through the tunnel to France in only half an hour. Ten minutes later she saw Dover Castle and the White Cliffs. And then the road went past the centre of the small town to Britain's busiest passenger port.

It was 12.30. Perfect timing! Claire got into the queue for the 13.15 ferry to Calais. On this Saturday morning all the people in south-east England seemed to be on their way to Calais. British people loved to go to Calais to buy the things that were cheaper there than in Britain. There were British supermarkets in Calais that sold wine, cigarettes – and British beer! Claire wasn't interested in those things, but she remembered the other things she had enjoyed on family trips to Britain's nearest neighbour – baguettes, orange lemonade and Camembert cheese.

But there was no time today to buy cheese when she got to the other side of the Channel. It was 250 miles, no, she had to think in kilometres now, *400 kilometres,* from Calais to Cologne.

The crossing to Calais went much too fast for Claire. Like many of the other people on the ferry she stood on the deck and took photos as "The Duchess of Kent" started its journey. She looked back towards the White Cliffs of Dover and the small town under the cliffs that had already been an important port over two thousand years ago, when the Romans were in Britain. She watched as Britain got smaller and smaller and the seagulls flew above the ferry. Then she went to the restaurant and had her last English meal for some time: fish and chips.

An hour later "The Duchess of Kent" arrived in the port of Calais. Claire wanted to stay and watch from the deck, but a loudspeaker voice was telling people to go down to their vehicles. Claire remembered where her motor bike was on the enormous ferry – Blue Deck. When she arrived in the ferry's "car park", the big doors at the front of the ship were already open and the first cars were leaving. But Claire didn't want to hurry. She had a long journey in front of her. She checked that "Susie", her Suzuki motor bike, was OK after the crossing. Then she put on her helmet and zipped up her leather jacket.

Then it happened – or didn't happen. The motor bike didn't start. "Oh no!" thought Claire. She tried again. Nothing.

Behind Claire another motorcyclist sounded his horn. The traffic lights near the big doors had been green for a long time now. All the cars had left the ferry. Claire got off her bike. She checked "Susie" again.

"What's the matter with you?" she thought. The other motorcyclist was still behind her. She looked at him.

"What's the problem?" he said.

"I don't know," said Claire.

The young man got off his big machine and took off his helmet. He looked fantastic!

"Hi! I'm Tim," he said.

"And this is my broken-down motor bike," said Claire.

"Hi, broken-down motor bike," said the young man and smiled at "Susie".

"Oh, I'm sorry, Tim. My name is Claire, Claire Hall. And, as I said before, this is my broken-down motor bike."

"Perhaps I can help," he said.

"Great!" said Claire.

Tim sat on Claire's motor bike. He tried to start the Suzuki, but nothing happened.

"I have an idea," he said.

Claire couldn't see exactly what the young man was doing. But a minute later her machine started.

"What was it?" asked Claire.

"Nothing really. Just a loose cable."

Tim smiled and opened his leather jacket.

"Where did I put my handkerchief?" he was saying while he felt in his leather jacket. His fingers were really dirty from checking Claire's motor bike.

Claire gave him her handkerchief. "Here, Tim. Take mine."

"But it'll get dirty," said Tim.

"That's OK." Claire smiled. Tim's help was more than worth a dirty handkerchief.

"Hey, you two," shouted an unfriendly voice. "Leave the ferry!"

"We should do what the seaman says," said Tim and smiled at Claire. While he put the dirty handkerchief back in his jacket, Claire saw that he was wearing a Manchester City shirt.

"What a coincidence!" said Claire. "I'm a Manchester City fan too."

"We fans stick together," said Tim.

"It's time to go!" shouted the angry seaman.

"Bye, Tim," Claire said.

"I'm sure we'll meet again one day," said Tim. "At a City match perhaps."

"I'm going to Cologne," said Claire quickly.

"What a coincidence, I'm going there too!"

"Get off the ferry – now!" roared the seaman.

Claire was surprised that the French customs officer stopped her. There weren't usually customs checks between England and France now.

"Where are you going?" asked the officer in very good English.

"To Cologne, in Germany."

"Take your panniers off the motor bike, please."

Claire was worried. Perhaps it was against the law to have ten bars of chocolate with you. They were for her father. It was very difficult for him to get *Cadbury's* chocolate in Germany. Claire's father liked living in Germany but he still had to have his English favourites. When he travelled to England, he always took an empty sports bag with him. On the way back to Germany it was full of English sweets, biscuits and lots of other nice things.

"Well, mademoiselle, what are you waiting for?" said the customs officer.

" I have lots of chocolate with me," Claire said.
The customs officer laughed. "We aren't looking for chocolate."
"What are you looking for?"
The customs officer didn't answer. He looked very serious.
"Take your panniers off the motor bike and follow me, please."

Lots of other motorcyclists were waiting in the customs shed. Customs officers were checking everybody's bags. Claire saw that Tim was sitting there too.
"Do you know what's happening?" Claire asked the young man, as a customs officer started unpacking her panniers. She checked all Claire's things, even her tube of toothpaste.
"I think they're looking for drugs," Tim said.
"How terrible!" said Claire.
"That's their job," said Tim.

Ten minutes later Claire and Tim left the customs shed. While they were putting their panniers back on their motor bikes, Tim asked Claire, "Why don't we travel to Cologne together?"
"But your bike is much bigger than mine. I'm too slow for you."
"Do you know the Ardennes? Or the Eifel?"
"I know the Eifel. When I visited my father two years ago, we had a trip there. There are lots of hills and small towns."
"And lots and lots of super roads for riding a motor bike. I'll show them to you."
Claire looked at her watch. It was three, no, four o'clock, French time. It was 400 kilometres to Cologne. She could be there in five hours on the motorway. She had promised her father on the phone not to travel at night. And he had told her that sunset tonight was at 9.30 pm. So she had enough time.

"OK, Tim. But you must promise one thing."
"I promise I'll go really slowly," laughed Tim.
"No, no, Tim. I must be in Cologne by 10 pm, German time, before it gets really dark. My father is waiting for me. And he'll be worried if I'm late."
"You'll be on time. I promise."

The Ardennes were fantastic. Claire had to stop again and again to enjoy the view. She took lots of photos. When they had a break three hours later in St Vith, a small town in the German-speaking part of Belgium, Claire phoned her father in Cologne.
"Hi, Dad. It's me, Claire."
"Hallo, Claire, my little girl."
"Little girls don't ride motor bikes, Dad. Look, I'm going to be in Cologne a little later than I planned."
"What's the matter? Are you having problems with your motor bike?"
"No, no, Dad. Everything is OK. I'm taking a different route, via the Ardennes and the Eifel. We'll – I mean *I'll* – be in Cologne at about 10 o'clock."
Claire's father laughed. "Who's 'we'?"
"I'll explain later, Dad. I have to phone Mum now."
"OK, Claire. See you soon."

Before Claire and Tim left St Vith, they ate chips from a chip shop, a *Fritüre*. Claire had never eaten such fantastic chips. Tim explained that the Belgians were chip experts. There was a Belgian who had invented a six-sided chip, he told Claire. Claire asked him if there were six-sided fish in the Belgian part of the North Sea. Tim laughed. "You're great fun, Claire."

Claire and Tim didn't stop again on the journey through the Eifel. Claire had no more film in her camera! They arrived in Cologne at 9.30 pm and stopped at *Neumarkt* to say goodbye. Tim had a hotel room near there. Claire's father lived on the other side of the Rhine in Merheim. Claire's father said Cologne people called it "Schääl Sick" – "the wrong side" – and Claire had to think of the people in Oxford who called Cambridge "The Other Place". Oxford, where she had had her morning break, seemed so far away now. And Chester seemed even further away.

"How long are you going to be in Cologne?" Tim asked her.

"A week."

"I'm here for four days."

"Perhaps we could meet for an ice-cream," Claire said.

"Great idea!" Tim looked very happy.

"You can phone me," said Claire.

"I will!"

Claire gave Tim her father's phone number in Merheim. Then she put her helmet on and rode away towards Deutz Bridge. In her mirror she saw that Tim was waving to her with the handkerchief she had given him in Calais.

"What a super day!" she thought.

CHAPTER THREE

As Claire was parking her motor bike outside her father's house, the door opened. Her father came towards her. He looked so happy.

"How long has it been?" he asked and took her in his arms.

"Careful, Dad. You're hurting me," said Claire.

"A year?"

"More than a year. It was New Year."

"Oh, Claire. Time goes so quickly."

"That's what mum said. Now, can you help me with my things?"

"Yes, of course."

Claire gave her father her bags.

"Can I leave 'Susie' here?" she asked.

"No problem."

Claire followed her father into the house. She suddenly realised how tired she was. The journey to Germany had been tougher than she had thought, although she had done lots of long trips on her days off from the restaurant. One day she had travelled to Brighton and back. When she arrived there, she sent a postcard to her Uncle Harry. It said, "Dear Uncle Harry, I'm following your advice and I'm practising riding my motor bike. Bye, Claire."

"What do you want to eat, Claire?"

"Nothing, thanks, Dad. I'm just tired."

"I could phone for a pizza. That won't take long."

Claire's father was a really bad cook. Apart from bacon and eggs, everything he cooked was a disaster. Claire remembered the two weeks when her father had "looked after" her and her brother because her mum was in hospital. That's why she said "yes" to the pizza idea.

Twenty minutes later Claire had had a shower and the pizza had arrived.
"Tell me, Claire, how was your journey?" her dad asked.
Claire didn't get far with her story. She felt so tired. And she had only got to her break in Oxford!
"We'll talk again tomorrow," said her father.
"Yes. Good night, Dad."

On Sunday Claire slept till 10 o'clock. When she woke up, she could hear her father in the kitchen. He seemed to be talking to himself.
"What's the matter?" she shouted.
"Nothing really. I've just burned the milk."
"Is breakfast ready?"
"It will be, when I've boiled some more milk. I thought you'd like some cocoa."
Claire got up quickly.
"If I let dad do it, I'll never get breakfast," she thought.
Her father was terrible at cooking, but he was great at planning trips. While they were having breakfast he told her what he had planned for Sunday.
"You've seen so many things in Cologne," he said. "That's why we're going to go by car to Hattingen and have afternoon coffee there. It isn't far from here."
"Hattingen?" said Claire.
"It's a small town on the Ruhr, with a lot of nice old buildings and some fantastic cafés."
"That sounds great, Dad," said Claire.

The next two days went so quickly. Claire's father had planned some super things. On the way home from Hattingen they stopped in Wuppertal and travelled on the famous *Schwebebahn*. Claire was shocked when she learned that a baby elephant – Tuffi – had fallen out of the *Schwebebahn* in 1950.

The next day they went to a super museum in Oberhausen. Claire found out that two hundred years ago the big cities of the Ruhr had just been villages and small towns. As a football fan Claire knew the names Dortmund, Bochum ("Not *Bockum*, Claire," her dad had said) and Schalke, of course. But she hadn't known that Schalke was just part of the city of Gelsenkirchen. Oh well, she couldn't know everything!

When the phone rang on Tuesday, Claire was watching TV. She was watching the *Tagesschau*, but it wasn't really a *show!* It was difficult to understand this news programme. Although Claire had been very good at German at school, she couldn't follow much of what the smart young man on TV was saying. Her father had told her not to worry. It was always like that, he said. There was a big difference between learning a language at school and living in the country where it was spoken. After seven years in Germany Mr Hall could now speak German really well. He was on the phone now. She heard him say his name, "Hall". It sounded very strange to her. In England you said your phone number or just "Hallo".
"Claire, it's for you," her father shouted.
"Who is it?"
"It's Tim."
"Oh, Tim!"

Claire got up quickly and took the phone from her father. She was so excited she was out of breath.

"Hallo."

"Hi, Claire, it's me, Tim. I'd like to ask you if we could have that ice-cream tomorrow."

"My dad wanted to take me to the chocolate museum tomorrow morning," said Claire and looked at her father. Of course she had told him about Tim. She had told him too that she'd like to see Tim again.

"And what are you doing in the afternoon?"

Claire asked her father what he had planned for the afternoon. When her father said, "Go on, meet Tim," she was so happy.

"OK, Tim, in the afternoon."

"I'll come at 3 o'clock, Claire. Is that OK?" asked Tim.

"Super!"

"Just tell me where your father lives."

Claire was so excited she couldn't think of the house number. So she said, "It's the house with the red door. I'll wait outside."

"I'll find you," said Tim

"See you tomorrow, Tim."

"Bye, Claire."

The next morning Claire and her father visited the chocolate museum in Cologne. "It isn't bad," her father had said. "But *Cadbury World* is better."

She was just watching a video about cocoa when somebody tapped her on the shoulder. She turned around to see who it was and recognised Tim.

"Tim?" was all she could say. She was so happy.

"Hallo, Mr Hall. I'm Tim, Tim Woodruff."

Tim was wearing a smart suit. His shirt seemed to be freshly ironed. He was even wearing a tie. Claire liked that.

"Hallo, Tim. My daughter has told me a lot about you." Claire's father looked at the young man carefully.

"I hope she has only told you good things." Tim smiled at Claire.

"Only the best. My daughter seems to like you," Claire's father said.

"Dad!" Claire shouted and went a little red.

"What are you doing in the chocolate museum?" Mr Hall asked Tim.

"I wanted to introduce myself before I kidnap your daughter."

"An invitation to have an ice-cream isn't kidnapping," Claire's father said.

"Mr Hall, I'll be very open with you. I have to go to Berlin tomorrow morning on business. And I'd like to know if your daughter ...," Tim said in a serious voice as he looked at Mr Hall. Then he turned to Claire. "... if you, Claire, could go there with me."

"That *does* sound like kidnapping," Mr Hall said.

When the Halls and Tim said goodbye that evening, no decision had been made. Although Claire was 17 and almost grown-up, Mr Hall still had the last word on some things. One of these was the trip to Berlin, and he told Tim this. He was responsible for his daughter while she was in Germany.

Claire thought her father was going to say "no". So she was very happy when at their evening meal – pizza from the pizza service – her father suddenly said, "OK. Fly to Berlin with Tim. He seems to be a nice young man. And he supports the right football team. You must just promise to look after yourself."
"Oh, Dad! You're fantastic!"

The next day Mr Hall took Claire to Cologne-Bonn airport. The Halls were a little late because of the traffic on the Cologne motorway ring. Mr Hall carried Claire's bag into the airport. Tim was waiting there nervously. He gave Claire her ticket and she checked her bag in. Then a loudspeaker voice asked all passengers on Deutsche BA Flight DI 7064 to Berlin to go to Gate D80. Claire had just enough time to give her dad a big kiss and whisper, "Thanks, Dad."
Later, in the queue for the security check, she turned around. Her dad was still watching. He waved to her, then walked away quickly.

An hour later Claire and Tim were in Berlin. After they had got their bags, they took a taxi to their hotel.
"How can you afford this, Tim?" Claire asked in the lift. "The flight for us both, this fantastic hotel?"
"Business, Claire, business."
"But a night here must cost a fortune!" said Claire.
"Yes," said Tim. "But I can earn two fortunes in a night!"

Claire spent a long time getting ready the next morning. When she went down for breakfast, Tim was already there. He was phoning and sounded angry. What was the matter? Claire was going to ask him soon.
But she forgot all this when she saw the breakfast buffet. Claire had never before seen a table that was so full of nice things. Fruit, many different cheeses, cold meats, bread, rolls, all just waiting for hungry mouths.
"And what's that?" she asked Tim and pointed to a small plate.
"That's salmon," said Tim.
"Oh." Claire gave him a kiss.

That day Claire said "Oh" very, very often. Not because of Berlin, but because of Tim. Of course Berlin was an exciting city. But what Tim had planned for her was even more exciting.

At 11 o'clock a taxi came to their hotel.
"Where are we going?" asked Claire.
"Shopping, Claire."

Ten minutes later Claire walked into a very expensive clothes shop.
"Are you sure we're in the right shop?" she asked Tim after she had tried on the fourth dress.
"Of course we are," said Tim.
"But why do I need such a fantastic dress?" asked Claire.
"We're going dancing this evening," said Tim. He took her in his arms and kissed her. Claire felt great. She was in love.

In another clothes shop they picked a smart business suit for Claire.
"And when should I wear this suit?"

"Now. You and I are going to have lunch together."

"But don't you have to work?"

"My meeting isn't till 3 o'clock."

But when Tim wanted to go into a jeweller's shop with Claire, she shook her head.

"No, Tim. You've already given me enough. I can't and won't take any more presents."

Tim looked at Claire for a long time.

"Look, Claire, I know what you're thinking. But you're wrong. I don't want to buy you. I just want to make you happy. I saw how much you enjoyed trying on all those nice clothes."

"Oh, Tim. We women enjoy trying on clothes. But it's different if somebody gives us all these expensive things as a present."

"OK, OK," said Tim.

Ten minutes later Tim went into a shop and bought himself some sunglasses. When Claire first saw him with them, she laughed and said, "You look like a criminal with those!"

Tim laughed back.

"I hope I look like a nice criminal."

After lunch in a very expensive restaurant Tim said goodbye to Claire. Before he went to his meeting, he gave her a small leather wallet.

"What's this?" asked Claire.

"Money."

"And why are you giving it to me?"

"Go shopping," Tim said.

"Tim!" Claire shouted. "You don't have to give me presents. I'm happy if I can be with you."

"I don't know how long my meeting will take. I could be very late. You can have a nice time with the money."

Claire took the leather wallet from Tim's hand.

"I'll show you that I don't need money to have a nice time. When we meet again, you can have all your money back!"

"Claire, I believe you," said Tim and got into the waiting taxi.

At 6 o'clock, with tired legs because she had walked through the *Tiergarten* to the Brandenburg Gate, Claire was back at the hotel. She looked in the wallet to see how much money Tim had given her. When she counted the money, she felt weak at the knees. She couldn't earn that much in a year at *Stringers.* Claire didn't understand how a young man like Tim could have so much money.

Tim had told Claire's father the day before how he earned his money. He looked for new employees for big companies.

"I'm a headhunter."

The name of the job sounded terrible to Claire. But Claire's father knew what Tim meant. "They even use the English word in German," he had said to Claire. And then he said to Tim, "You must earn a lot of money."

"I can't complain," Tim had said.

Tim came back very late from his business meeting. Although he seemed to be very tired, they were still going dancing. While Tim had a shower, Claire changed. The dress was really fantastic. Everybody was going to look at her tonight.

When the two young people were sitting in the taxi to the disco, Claire couldn't wait any longer.
"Tim," she said, "I have a problem."
"Tell me what it is and I'll solve it," said Tim.
"Where do you get so much money?"
"But Claire, I told you yesterday."
"But I still don't understand."
"What don't you understand?"
"I don't understand how you can earn so much money."
"I'm just really good at my job."
"But what do you do exactly?"
"I can't really talk about it," said Tim.

But then, back at the hotel three hours later, Tim asked her, "Would you really like to know the truth about my job?"
"I want to know everything about you," said Claire and looked into Tim's beautiful eyes.
And Tim started to explain what kind of job he really had. After the first words, Claire went very, very pale.

CHAPTER FOUR

In early October Claire visited her father for the second time since the summer. Of course Mr Hall was very pleased to see his daughter again. But he wondered why Claire visited him so often. Was it really because she liked riding her motor bike so much? Mr Hall didn't think so. You could ride a motor bike in England too. In early October the weather was usually better in England than in Germany. The first snow had already fallen in the Eifel. They had both seen the pictures on TV the evening before.

Now they were sitting at the breakfast table. Claire was making sandwiches for the journey back to Chester.

"Claire, I'm worried," Mr Hall said.

"Dad, you mustn't get worried. The weather forecast says there'll be no snow today."

"Claire, I'm not worried about the weather."

"What are you worried about then?"

"You were so quiet this weekend."

Claire laughed. "Dad, I've just started college. I have lots on my mind."

"Well, tell me what's on your mind."

Claire looked at her father for a long time. "Dad," she said, "I have to learn to solve my problems myself."

"And do you have problems?" Mr Hall wanted to know.

"Of course not."

"Claire, what's the matter with you? You're so different."

"It's nothing, Dad. I just have to think about lots of different things at the moment. College is the start of my future. If I do something wrong now, it will affect my whole life."

"Claire, you know I'll always be there for you," Mr Hall said.

"That's what Uncle Harry said," Claire laughed. "He gave me some good advice. You know Uncle Harry always likes to give advice."

Mr Hall laughed.

"Yes, I know."

An hour later Claire left. She promised to phone her father as soon as she was back in Chester.

"And please ride carefully," he said as she left.

"I always ride carefully," said Claire.

"What about the ticket you got last month for going too fast?"

Claire went a little red. "I just didn't see the sign, Dad. I don't usually go too fast."

Before Claire put her helmet on, Mr Hall asked her a last question. He had wanted to ask it all weekend.

"What about Tim? Are you still friends? You've told me nothing about him."

"Yes, we're still friends," was all Claire said.

"Say hallo to him from me," said Mr Hall.

"I'll do that, Dad."

"And phone when you're back in Chester."

"I promise, Dad."

As Claire slowly rode away, Mr Hall felt a little sad. His little girl had changed so much in the last months. It couldn't be because of Tim. Mr Hall thought he was a responsible and polite young man, although it was a bit strange that he had invited Claire to go to Berlin with him after such a short time. That's what Claire's mother thought too. No, Mr Hall was sure Claire had other problems. And they had nothing to do with starting college. He knew that. Something was the matter with his little girl.

Claire didn't take the quickest route to England. She didn't follow the A4 motorway to Aachen, but rode north to Duisburg. She was going to an old warehouse in the port. A man was waiting there for her. She only knew him as Bill. Claire didn't think Bill was English. And she was sure he wasn't an American. He spoke English with an accent. It wasn't Scottish or Irish, and it certainly wasn't Welsh. Claire knew the Welsh accent. Chester was very near Wales. Some of Claire's old school friends, Evan Parry, for example, came from Wales.

Bill gave Claire the parcel. She put it under the seat of her motor bike.

"Say hallo to Tim for me," Bill said as she left.

"OK," said Claire.

"Tell him that the weather is getting better."

"Where do you mean?" asked Claire. "The weather in Germany or in England?"

"Don't ask so many questions, girl. Just tell Tim that the weather is getting better. He'll understand."

Claire didn't answer. She didn't like Bill. He was always unfriendly to her.

"Do you understand, girl?"

"Yes, I do."

"Then repeat my message for Tim."

"The weather is getting better."

"Exactly, girl, exactly. And now go! Tim is waiting for the parcel."

But the weather didn't get better, it got worse. Just before Claire crossed the border at Venlo, it started to rain. Claire had to stop and put her rain gear on. But she was pleased about the rain. There weren't usually customs checks in bad weather. Claire was really worried about customs checks. What if the parcel was found in a customs check? Claire didn't want to think about it.

"Why am I doing this?" she asked herself. "I shouldn't do this. And I shouldn't do this for him."

Under her seat Claire was carrying drugs. There were two kilos of heroin in the parcel.

Claire remembered the evening in Berlin when Tim told her how he earned his money. At first she didn't want to believe him. You only heard about drugs in crime films. Then she understood that Tim wasn't joking. He was a dealer. He earned a lot of money from dealing in drugs.

"I'm going to the police," Claire said.

"No, no, Claire. Please don't do that!"

"It's against the law to deal in drugs!"

"Yes, I know."

"Why do you do it then?"

"I'm forced to do it."

"Tim, nobody can be forced to deal in drugs."

"Yes, they can, Claire. I'm forced to do it. I can't just stop."

"You could go to the police," Claire said.

"No, Claire, no, I can't. They'll kill me."

"Tim, I don't understand you. The police don't kill drugs dealers."

"Oh, Claire, not the police. The Mafia is behind the drugs trade. And if I go to the police, they'll send somebody to kill me."

"Oh no!"

Claire was more worried about Tim than frightened of the Mafia. She didn't know how she could live without him. She had only known him for three days, but she loved him. She wanted to be together forever with Tim.

Claire couldn't sleep. At school she had learned that drugs cause addiction. And at the end of addiction was death. But she didn't want Tim to be killed. Claire had to make a terrible decision.

They talked again at – a very late! – breakfast.

"Drugs are terrible. You're right," said Tim. "But nobody is forced to take drugs. It's like TV. There are good programmes and bad programmes. Nobody is forced to watch a bad programme."

"TV isn't a drug!" shouted Claire. She was very angry.

"OK, OK. But if I smuggle drugs to England, I'm not killing anybody. The people kill themselves. They're the ones who take drugs."

Although Claire didn't agree with Tim, she didn't go to the police. Tim had to live! But the price was very high for Claire. She had terrible problems with her conscience. Again and again she asked herself if she had really done the right thing.

In terrible rain Claire rode her motor bike across Holland and Belgium to Ostend. She stayed away from Calais because there were too often customs checks there or at the border between Belgium and France.

Two years ago Tim had been caught with drugs in a check in Calais.

"It wasn't much," he said. "I'm glad it wasn't heroin. For smuggling heroin you have to go to prison."

And so Tim only got a suspended sentence. And he had to work in a hospital for drug addicts. Tim talked about his sentence the way other people talked about a parking ticket.

"But why didn't you stop smuggling?" Claire asked.

"I couldn't. My bosses are real criminals. People who don't follow the rules are ... No, Claire, I won't tell you what they do with traitors. It's too terrible."

"But now you've told me what work you do. Aren't you a traitor too?" Claire asked Tim.

"Yes, ... no, ... well, yes. But, Claire, I trust you. I know that you won't betray me. If what I've told you stays our secret, then nothing can happen to me." Tim took Claire's hands. She saw he was shaking.

Tim told Claire more and more about his life as a drugs dealer. His bosses weren't very happy about his sentence for smuggling drugs. Tim had to show he was still a good worker.

"What did you have to do?" asked Claire.

"I had to find new drugs couriers."

"And did you find some?"

"Yes," is all Tim said.

"Who?"

"No, Claire, I can't tell you."

"But you said you trusted me."

Claire looked at Tim for a long time.

"It's so terrible." Tim started to cry quietly.

"What's the matter?"

"I've persuaded friends to work as drugs couriers. Do you understand? My friends have become criminals because of me. Some of these friends haven't only carried drugs, they've taken drugs themselves."

"Oh, Tim, that's terrible!"

Tim told Claire that his bosses were soon very pleased with him. He soon doubled the number of couriers. Because of this he had a better job now. He was no longer a courier.

"They made me the boss for the North of England."

Claire remembered who "they" were.

"Then you're a Mafia boss. You don't just work for the gang. You're one of them!"

"No, Claire, no! I'm forced to do it. You must believe me!"

"You do it for the money."

"No, Claire, no."

"You say you're forced, but you take the money."

"I have to take the money," Tim said in a quiet voice.

"You have to? Have to? You don't have to take it!" Claire shouted at Tim.

"Claire, you have no idea what the Mafia is. If I don't take the money, they won't trust me. And if the Mafia doesn't

trust you, you're as good as dead. I have to play the game to survive. So I have to take the money too."

Claire wished Tim would stop talking about the Mafia. It was terrible to think that the man she loved was involved with those terrible people.

Two days later Claire and Tim said goodbye at Cologne-Bonn airport. Tim had to go back to England, for "business". His motor bike was with a friend in Cologne. Just before he left, Claire said, "Why don't I help you with your business?"

"Claire, what did you say?"

"I'd like to help you."

"Claire, ... I don't know what to say."

"I'll help you," Claire said.

She had thought a long time about this decision. She knew that dealing in drugs was a terrible crime. But she felt too that Tim needed her help. The evening before he had told her that he had "lost" many of his couriers. He would soon be in trouble with the Mafia again.

"Claire, I like you so much. I don't want you to have anything to do with my business!"

Claire looked at Tim for a long time.

"Tim, I know. That's why I'm offering you my help."

Tim couldn't answer.

"You know what people promise when they get married," Claire said.

"In good times and bad times?"

"Yes, Tim. Even if we aren't married, I'd like to help you in bad times. Because I love you." Claire smiled. "And two Manchester City fans like us should stick together – forever."

"Oh, Claire, you're so fantastic."

Claire often met Tim in the weeks after that. They never talked about his business. Sometimes he visited her at her mother's house, sometimes she went to his house. He lived alone in a large house in the country near Manchester.

Then at a match between City and United Tim asked her the question.
"Can you travel to Germany for me?"
And Claire said yes. There was no other answer for her. She wanted to help Tim.

So in early September her father heard that she was going to visit him again. On the way home from Cologne she picked up one of the parcels for the first time. She was so nervous that she couldn't lift her motor bike seat. And again and again she used the wrong name for Bill and called him Will. He looked very angry and said, "I'm Bill, do you understand? Bill."
"Sorry, Will."
She hated that first trip and told Tim that she wanted to stop being a courier.
Tim looked sad. "I thought you loved me," he said.

And now this was her second trip for Tim. When Claire left the ferry in Dover, she was really nervous. Then it happened. As she rode past the customs building, her motor bike broke down. It stuttered, then it was quiet. Claire's heart was in her mouth.
"Can I help you?" A customs officer came out of the building.
"No, no, it's OK, thank you," said Claire. She couldn't bring herself to look at the helpful officer. She was sure that he knew what was under the seat of her motor bike.

"I ride a motor bike myself," said the young man.

Claire didn't know what to say.

"It's probably only a small thing."

"I th-think so t-too," stuttered Claire.

"Push your motor bike into our shed."

"The customs shed?" asked Claire.

"Yes, it's over there." Claire looked. She saw the big open doors and the words "Customs Inspection".

"I'm sure I can repair it myself," said Claire.

"Do you have tools with you?"

"Er, no."

"See. But there are lots of tools in our shed."

"Really?"

Claire was so nervous she couldn't speak. Her mouth was very dry and she was sweating terribly.

"Yes, we have some very good tools in the shed," said the officer. "We need them when we check cars for drugs, you see."

Claire was so frightened she felt dizzy. She had to hold onto her machine.

"Don't worry. We'll soon fix your motor bike."

But Claire *was* worried. She had become a criminal and she couldn't stop if she didn't want to lose the man she loved.

CHAPTER FIVE

"Ho, ho, ho, on this really cold day. It's 9 o'clock and there's snow on the ground! The weather forecast looks good. All we need now is the weekend. And, talking of the weekend, here on Radio Chester everything will be about Father Christmas, our old friend Santa Claus, because it's only two weeks till Christmas now. That's why the next song is "Santa Claus is coming to town!" from good old Frankie Boy Sinatra."

It wasn't very busy this Friday in *Stringers Restaurant.* It was a terribly cold morning. Not even the students at Brookland School wanted to come over and get a nice, hot hamburger. The only people in the restaurant were Claire and Mr Stringer. They were sitting at a table together. Claire had sat at this same table five months ago with Andrew Wilson. Those five months felt like a lifetime to her.

"Claire, I'm worried about you," said Mr Stringer.

"Oh, Mr Stringer, you needn't. I'm OK."

"Are you having problems at the college?"

"No, Mr Stringer. I really enjoy it there."

"Problems with your father?"

"No, Mr Stringer. My father and I get on really well."

"Oh, yes. You visit him every month now. What does your mother say about that?"

"She's pleased."

"Claire, girl, something is worrying you!" The owner of the restaurant looked at her thoughtfully.

Claire pointed to the newspaper on the table.

"Andrew is dead."

"Andrew?"

"Andrew Wilson."

Mr Stringer looked at the photo in the paper. "I've seen him before."

"Do you remember my last day at work in the summer? It was that terribly hot day. The next morning I went to Germany on my motor bike. I sat and talked to Andrew here in the restaurant. He had chips and a hamburger, I had a cola. Then he had some more chips."

Mr Stringer thought for a moment.

"Yes, that strange young man. I remember now. He didn't look OK even then. What did he die of?"

"Drugs," was all Claire said.

Mr Stringer shook his head. "Your friend took drugs? How terrible!"

"Yes, Mr Stringer, he took drugs. He died from an overdose of heroin."

"Did you know he took drugs?"

Claire shook her head. "Of course not."

"Claire, I'm an old man. Perhaps a lot of what I say sounds old-fashioned. But believe me. If you know a drug addict, you must help him or her. You don't have to go to the police. There are other places. Talk to the parents, talk to the friends. Talk to the teachers. Drug addicts need help. They can't solve their problems alone. Somebody who takes drugs is ill."

"Andrew was such fun." Claire started to cry.

"Claire, don't cry."

"Oh, Mr Stringer, I feel so guilty."

"But why? You didn't know he was ill. You couldn't help him."

Claire dried her eyes. She felt terrible.

"Another coffee?" asked Mr Stringer and got up.

"I'd like a hot cocoa now. I still have to ride my motor bike."

"Not in this weather, Claire. It's winter. There's snow on the ground and the roads are icy."

"I know," Claire said.

"What's so important?"

"I'm visiting my boyfriend," said Claire.

"Timmy?"

"Yes, Mr Stringer, I'm visiting Tim." Of course Claire had told Mr Stringer about her boyfriend. The two of them had eaten in the restaurant one evening too.

"Why don't you visit Tim later? In this weather a trip on a motor bike is very, very dangerous. I'm sure Tim doesn't want you to have an accident."

"I have to go, Mr Stringer. I have to." Claire quickly got up. She took her jacket and her helmet.

"What about your cocoa?"

"Perhaps I'll have one when I come back."

Mr Stringer watched Claire go. The girl had changed a lot in the last months. She wasn't as happy as in the summer. Mr Stringer hadn't heard Claire laugh in the last four weeks. So Claire's problems couldn't have anything to do with the death of Andrew Wilson.

Claire rode especially carefully. She couldn't risk an accident. In the panniers of her motor bike she had four kilos of heroin. But Claire hadn't brought the drugs herself from Germany to England.
"You can't do that now," Tim had told her. "People notice motorcyclists in the winter."

So for two months it had been Claire's job to transport the heroin when it arrived in England. Sometimes she went to Dover for Tim, sometimes she went to Harwich. She had been to Hull three times. And every time she came back to Tim with the kilos of heroin. The drugs had been brought by other couriers to England.
"You do your job really well, Claire," Tim said.
But Claire hated her job.

Tim lived near Manchester. On this Friday morning the road to Manchester seemed to be full of delivery vans. Like the Bedford Blitz with the words *Campbell's Tomato Soup* on it. For ten kilometres the van had been behind Claire. When she moved right to overtake, the Bedford Blitz followed her. But in spite of the four kilos of heroin in her panniers Claire didn't worry about the van.

She thought about Andrew Wilson. Claire knew him from school. Andrew had been a terrible boy then. At first Claire was frightened of the new boy in the class. He often put chewing gum in girls' hair. When he tried to do it to her, Claire scratched him very badly with her comb. She had got into a lot of trouble at school because of this.

Although it was Claire who got into trouble, Andrew stopped his chewing gum attacks. Claire and Andrew became friends. They swapped sandwiches in the breaks. And they did their homework together some evenings.

That all finished when Andrew had to go to another school. He had been caught in the toilets again with cigarettes. He was 13 at the time.
Soon after the Wilson family went to London and the contact between Andrew and Claire stopped. Claire was sad when Andrew didn't answer any of her three letters.

A year ago Andrew had come back to Chester. Claire wasn't sure if he had finished school. When she asked him about it, Andrew laughed. "School, stupid school!" he said. "The best school is life. So I live!"
Claire didn't agree with Andrew. School wasn't always easy, but it was very important.

When Claire left the M56 motorway just before Manchester, the *Campbell's Tomato Soup* delivery van was no longer following her. There was a green car behind her now. A woman was driving it. The next time Claire had to stop, she looked back. The woman was just staring at the traffic lights. Claire wasn't worried about the car. Tim had told her to watch out for people following her, but this woman wasn't a problem. Claire was sure of that.

Tim's house was on the edge of the city. There were tall hedges next to the road. There was snow on the hedges and on the roofs of the houses too. Claire rode slowly towards Tim's house. She was looking up at Tim's bathroom window. The bathroom window was a signal. If it was open, everything was OK. If the window was closed, Claire had to ride away.
"If the window is closed," Tim had said, "it means the police are near here. And I don't want you to be arrested."

On this winter morning the bathroom window was open. Claire rode slowly through the gate. Tim's car was in front of the garage. Claire parked her motor bike behind it.
"Hi, Claire!" Tim shouted from the front door. He had heard her coming, of course.
"Hallo, Tim, can you help me?" said Claire.
"What with?"
"I can't get the panniers off."
"Of course, Claire."
Tim was wearing jeans and a Manchester City sweatshirt.
"They must have stuck because it's so cold," said Claire.
"What about a new motor bike?" said Tim.
"Oh, Tim, I don't need a new motor bike."
"Yes, you do, Claire. I want to say thank you for your help. You do your job really well."

Five minutes later they were having a cup of tea in Tim's living-room. The panniers were next to the table.
"Don't you want to check the goods?" asked Claire.
"I trust you Claire."
"I know," said Claire and went a little red. "But can you trust the courier who brought the drugs to England?"
"You're worse than my bosses," said Tim. "OK, I'll check it."

Tim got a small box. There were some test tubes in it and three small bottles of chemicals. Tim opened the parcel.

At that moment there was a bang, and the living-room was suddenly full of light. Claire had instinctively closed her eyes when she heard the bang.
"Police!" voices shouted. "On the ground!"
"Put your hands behind your back!"
Claire did what the voices said. Then she felt the handcuffs.

"Hallo, Mr Woodruff," said a friendly voice. "Let me introduce myself. I'm Chief Inspector Mary Coltrane, drug squad."
Claire opened her eyes. She couldn't see much. Tim was lying next to her on the ground. He had handcuffs on too.
"Police bastards!" shouted Tim.

"Not bastards, drug squad!"
"Police bastards!" shouted Tim.
"Mr Woodruff, we have you at last."
"You have nothing!" shouted Tim.
"Mr Woodruff, shouting won't help. We know that you deal in drugs! Or what's in these parcels here on the table?"
"Police bastards!"
"Help them to get up," the friendly voice said.
Before Claire knew what was happening to her, she was pulled up. Almost at the same moment she was sitting on a chair. Tim was sitting next to her.
The house was full of police. Men with bulletproof vests and pistols in their hands were all around the room. Two officers were taking photos. And there was a woman too. Claire recognised her. It was the woman from the green car.
"And you, Claire? What do you have to say to all this?" asked Chief Inspector Coltrane.
"I'm glad that it's over," said Claire.
"Police bastards!" shouted Tim.
"Well, Mr Woodruff, we too are glad that it's over. You won't smuggle any drugs for the next twenty years. You'll sit in prison and have a lot of time to think."
" I have nothing to do with drugs!" shouted Tim.
"No? We've heard a different story."
"It's all lies. I don't deal in drugs!"
"And what's this?" The drugs officer pointed to the parcel with the heroin.
Tim laughed. "The girl brought it to me. Ask the girl why she did that."
The woman looked at Claire.
"Tim, your lies won't help you now. I betrayed you," Claire said with a dry mouth.

"You?" Tim turned his head. "You betrayed me?"

"Yes, Mr Woodruff. This girl was very brave and came to us. She told us all about your dirty business. And she said she wanted to help us arrest you."

"I had to do it, Tim. Dealing in drugs is a crime. Drugs kill. I didn't want to be part of it."

Chief Inspector Coltrane's mobile rang. "What's the news?" she asked. Then she said, "Great!" and closed her mobile.

"Mr Woodruff, since Miss Hall came to us two months ago, we've been watching you and your gang. I've just heard that all the members of the gang have been arrested."

Chief Inspector Coltrane took off Claire's handcuffs.

"Well done, Claire!" she said.

The next day Claire and her parents were sitting in the garden together. Mr Hall had got the first plane to Manchester when he heard the news. Chief Inspector Coltrane was there too. The Halls listened as Claire told them what had happened since the summer. She said that going to the police had been very dangerous.

"Yes, it was," said Chief Inspector Coltrane. "But we looked after your daughter."

"You were wrong to become a drugs courier," said Claire's mother. "It was a terrible thing to do. But you did the right thing in the end, and we're proud of you for that."

"Yes," said her father. "It can't have been easy for you to betray Tim."

"I had to do it, Dad," said Claire. "Drugs are bad. But I've lost the man I thought I loved."

Chief Inspector Coltrane explained to Claire's parents that Tim was not only a member of the gang. He was the boss.

"And I thought he was a nice young man," her father said.

"Mr Hall, gangsters like him aren't easy to see through. Your daughter realised just in time."
Chief Inspector Coltrane turned to Claire.
"Claire, what I have to tell you now isn't very nice. You see, Woodruff told us everything last night. He told us he had long wanted to have you as a courier. When your motor bike didn't start on the ferry, it was because Woodruff had done something to it. He followed you by motor bike from Chester. He had heard from your old friend Andrew Wilson that you had a father in Germany. A nice, young woman was the perfect drugs courier for him."
She took Claire's hand. The girl was smiling bravely, although there were tears in her eyes.
"I'm sorry, Claire."
Claire looked at her parents and Chief Inspector Coltrane. It was worse than she had thought. Meeting "headhunter" Tim Woodruff on the ferry hadn't been a coincidence. And what about the Manchester City shirt he had been wearing? That was probably part of his plan too.
Claire laughed. She still had her sense of humour.
"It's a terrible pity," she said. "And he was a City fan too – or so he said. We should have been together forever."

VOCABULARY

Abbreviations: s.p. = simple past (einfache Vergangenheit)
p.p. = past participle (Partizip Perfekt)

A

accident ['æksɪdənt] Unfall
across [ə'krɒs] (quer) durch, über
addiction [ə'dɪkʃn] Sucht
advice [əd'vaɪs] Rat, Ratschläge
affect [ə'fekt] sich auswirken auf
afford [ə'fɔːd] sich leisten
after that [ɑːftə'ðæt] danach
agree [ə'griː] übereinstimmen
although [ɔːl'ðəʊ] obwohl
apart from [ə'pɑːtfrəm] abgesehen von
Ardennes [ɑː'den] Ardennen
army ['ɑːmi] Armee, Heer
arrest [ə'rest] verhaften
at first [ət'fɜːst] zunächst
at last [ət'lɑːst] endlich
attack [ə'tæk] Angriff

B

back [bæk] Rücken
bang [bæŋ] Knall
bar [bɑː] Riegel
barbecue ['bɑːbɪkjuː] Grill
bastard ['bɑːstəd] *hier etwa:* Schwein, Schweinehund
beer [bɪə] Bier
Belgian ['beldʒən] belgisch
Belgium ['beldʒəm] Belgien
betray [bɪ'treɪ] verraten
big wheel [bɪg'wiːl] Riesenrad
biscuit ['bɪskɪt] Keks
boil [bɔɪl] kochen
border ['bɔːdə] Grenze
brave [breɪv] mutig
break down [breɪk'daʊn] eine Panne haben
breath [breθ]: **out of breath** außer Atem
broke down [brəʊk'daʊn] s.p. von **break down**
broken-down [brəʊkən'daʊn] kaputt
buffet ['bʊfeɪ] Büffet
building ['bɪldɪŋ] Gebäude
bulletproof vest ['bʊlɪtpruːf'vest] kugelsichere Weste
burn [bɜːn] anbrennen lassen
business ['bɪznəs] Geschäft; **on business** geschäftlich

C

cable ['keɪbl] Kabel
canal [kə'næl] Kanal
cash [kæʃ] (gegen Bargeld) einlösen
catch [kætʃ] fangen, verhaften
caught [kɔːt] s.p. von **catch**
cause [kɔːz] verursachen
certainly ['sɜːtnli] bestimmt
change [tʃeɪndʒ] sich umziehen
Channel Tunnel ['tʃænl'tʌnl] Kanaltunnel
check [tʃek] Kontrolle
check in [tʃek'ɪn] einchecken
chemical ['kemɪkl] Chemikalie
Chief Inspector [tʃiːfɪn'spektə] Hauptkommissar/in
Christmas ['krɪsməs] Weihnachten
cigarette [sɪgə'ret] Zigarette
cliff [klɪf] Klippe
coach [kəʊtʃ] Trainer/in
cocoa ['kəʊkəʊ] Kakao
coincidence [kəʊ'ɪnsɪdəns] Zufall
cold meats [kəʊld'miːts] Aufschnitt

collapse [kə'læps] zusammenbrechen
college ['kɒlɪdʒ] Berufsschule, Fach(hoch)schule; College (Teil einer Hochschule)
Cologne [kə'ləʊn] Köln
comb [kəʊm] Kamm
complain [kəm'pleɪn] sich beschweren
conscience ['kɒnʃəns] Gewissen
contact ['kɒntækt] Kontakt
continue [kən'tɪnju:] fortsetzen
cook [kʊk] Koch/Köchin
could(n't) ['kʊdnt] s.p. von **can('t)**
courier ['kʊrɪə] Kurier/in
criminal ['krɪmɪnl] Verbrecher/in
crossing ['krɒsɪŋ] Überfahrt
customs ['kʌstəmz] Zoll; **customs shed** Zollhalle

D
deal (in) [di:l] handeln (mit)
dealer ['di:lə] Händler/in, Dealer/in
death [deθ] Tod
decision [dɪ'sɪʒn] Entscheidung
deck [dek] Deck
delivery van [dɪ'lɪvəri'væn] Lieferwagen
detour ['di:tʊə] Umweg
difference ['dɪfrəns] Unterschied
dirty ['dɜ:ti] schmutzig
disaster [dɪ'zɑ:stə] Desaster
divorced [dɪ'vɔ:st] geschieden
dizzy ['dɪzi] schwindelig
double ['dʌbl] verdoppeln
dress [dres] Kleid
drug addict ['drʌg'ædɪkt] Drogensüchtige/r
drug squad ['drʌgskwɒd] Drogenfahndung
drugs trade ['drʌgztreɪd] Drogenhandel
dry [draɪ] trocken

E
earn [ɜ:n] verdienen
edge [edʒ] Rand
education [edʒu'keɪʃn] Ausbildung
elephant ['elɪfənt] Elefant
employee [ɪm'plɔɪi:] Angestellte/r
end [end] Ende; **in the end** am Ende
enormous [ɪ'nɔ:məs] riesig
even if ['i:vən'ɪf] auch wenn
exactly [ɪg'zæktli] genau; gerade
excited [ɪk'saɪtɪd] aufgeregt
exhibition ['eksɪ'bɪʃn] Ausstellung
expert ['ekspɜ:t] Experte/Expertin
eye [aɪ] Auge

F
fantastic [fæn'tæstɪk] fantastisch
Father Christmas ['fɑ:ðə'krɪsməs] der Weihnachtsmann
ferry ['feri] Fähre
fix [fɪks] in Ordnung bringen
flew [flu:] s.p. von **fly**
flight [flaɪt] Flug
fly [flaɪ] fliegen
force [fɔ:s] zwingen
forecast ['fɔ:kɑ:st]**: weather forecast** Wettervorhersage
forever [fər'evə] für immer
fortune ['fɔ:tʃu:n] Vermögen
France [frɑ:ns] Frankreich
freshly ironed ['freʃli'aɪənd] frisch gebügelt
further ['fɜ:ðə] weiter

G
gang [gæŋ] Gang, Bande
German-speaking ['dʒɜ:mənspi:kɪŋ] deutschsprachig
get married [get'mærid] heiraten
get off [get'ɒf] absteigen; losmachen
get on [get'ɒn]**: we get on really well** wir verstehen uns wirklich gut

get ready [get'redi] sich fertig machen
get up [get'ʌp] sich erheben
ghost train ['gəʊsttreɪn] Geisterbahn
glad [glæd]: **I'm glad** ich bin froh
goods [gʊdz] Ware
ground [graʊnd] (Erd-)Boden
grown-up [grəʊn'ʌp] erwachsen
guilty ['gɪlti] schuldig

H
had finished [hæd'fɪnɪʃt]: **she had finished** sie hatte beendet/aufgehört
handcuffs ['hændkʌfs] Handschellen
handkerchief ['hæŋkətʃɪf] Taschentuch
head [hed] Kopf
headhunter ['hedhʌntə] Headhunter/in, „Kopfjäger/in" (= jemand, der Arbeitskräfte abwirbt)
heart [hɑ:t]: **her heart was in her mouth** das Herz schlug ihr bis zum Hals
hedge [hedʒ] Hecke
held [held] s.p. von **hold**
helmet ['helmɪt] Helm
heroin ['herəʊɪn] Heroin
hold [həʊld] halten
hold onto [həʊld'ɒntə] sich festhalten an
horn [hɔ:n]: **sound the horn** hupen

I
icy ['aɪsi] glatt
inspection [ɪn'spekʃn] Kontrolle, Untersuchung
instinctively [ɪn'stɪŋktɪvli] instinktiv
introduce [ɪntrə'dju:s] vorstellen
invent [ɪn'vent] erfinden
invitation [ɪnvɪ'teɪʃn] Einladung
invite [ɪn'vaɪt] einladen
involved [ɪn'vɒlvd]: **he was involved with** er hatte mit … zu tun

J
jacket potato ['dʒækɪtpə'teɪtəʊ] Folienkartoffel
jeweller ['dʒu:ələ]: **jeweller's shop** Juwelier(laden)
junior national championships ['dʒu:niə'næʃnəl'tʃæmpiənʃɪps] Landesmeisterschaft der Junioren

K
kidnap ['kɪdnæp] entführen
kill [kɪl] töten
kilo ['ki:ləʊ] Kilo
kind of [kaɪndəv] Art

L
law [lɔ:] Gesetz
lawn [lɔ:n] Rasen
leather jacket ['leðədʒækɪt] Lederjacke
lend [lend] leihen
lent [lent] s.p. von **lend**
lie [laɪ] Lüge
lifetime ['laɪftaɪm]: **a lifetime** ein Leben lang
lift [lɪft] Fahrstuhl
lift [lɪft] heben
little ['lɪtl] klein
loose [lu:s] locker
loudspeaker [laʊd'spi:kə] Lautsprecher
love [lʌv]: **she was in love** sie war verliebt

M
machine [mə'ʃi:n] Maschine
married ['mærid] verheiratet
maybe ['meɪbi] vielleicht

mechanic [mə'kænɪk] Mechaniker/in
medal ['medl] Medaille
meeting ['mi:tɪŋ] Besprechung, Konferenz
mile [maɪl] Meile
mind [maɪnd]**: I have lots on my mind** ich habe viel im Kopf
mobile (phone) ['məʊbaɪl] Mobiltelefon, Handy
motor bike ['məʊtəbaɪk] Motorrad
motorcyclist ['məʊtəsaɪklɪst] Motorradfahrer/in
motorway ['məʊtəweɪ] Autobahn
mouth [maʊθ] Mund
move [mu:v] sich bewegen
mow [məʊ] mähen

N
notice ['nəʊtɪs] bemerken

O
off [ɒf]**: day off** freier Tag
offer ['ɒfə] anbieten
old-fashioned [əʊld'fæʃnd] altmodisch
Olympic [ə'lɪmpɪk] olympisch
onto ['ɒntə] auf (… hinauf/herauf)
order ['ɔ:də] bestellen
Ostend [ɒst'end] Ostende
overdose ['əʊvədəʊs] Überdosis
overtake [əʊvə'teɪk] überholen
owner ['əʊnə] Besitzer/in

P
pack [pæk] packen
pale [peɪl] blass
pannier ['pæniə] Motorradkoffer
parcel ['pɑ:sl] Paket
passenger ['pæsɪndʒə] Passagier/in
persuade [pə'sweɪd] überreden
pick up [pɪk'ʌp] abholen
pistol ['pɪstl] Pistole
pleased [pli:zd] zufrieden; erfreut
point to ['pɔɪnttə] zeigen auf
practise ['præktɪs] üben, trainieren
probably ['prɒbəbli] wahrscheinlich
promise ['prɒmɪs] versprechen
put on [pʊt'ɒn] aufsetzen

Q
quick [kwɪk] schnell

R
rain [reɪn] Regen
rain gear ['reɪngɪə] Regensachen
rang [ræŋ] s.p. von **ring**
ready ['redi] bereit, fertig
real ['ri:əl] echt
realise ['ri:əlaɪz]**: she realised** ihr wurde klar
recognise ['rekəgnaɪz] erkennen
repeat [rɪ'pi:t] wiederholen
responsible [rɪ'spɒnsəbl] verantwortlich; verantwortungsbewusst
Rhine [raɪn] Rhein
rider ['raɪdə] (Motorrad-)Fahrer/in
ring [rɪŋ] klingeln, läuten
ring [rɪŋ] Ring
risk [rɪsk] riskieren
rival ['raɪvl] Rivale/Rivalin
roar [rɔ:] aufheulen; brüllen
roller coaster ['rəʊləkəʊstə] Achterbahn
Roman ['rəʊmən] Römer/in
roof [ru:f] Dach
route [ru:t] Strecke
runner ['rʌnə] Läufer/in

S
salmon ['sæmən] Lachs
Santa Claus ['sæntəklɔ:z] der Weihnachtsmann (*eigentlich:* Sankt Nikolaus)
scratch [skrætʃ] kratzen
seagull ['si:gʌl] Möwe
seaman ['si:mən] Seemann

seat [si:t] Sitz
secret ['si:krət] Geheimnis
secretarial course [sekrə'teəriəlkɔ:s] Lehrgang für Sekretäre/ Sekretärinnen
security check [sɪ'kjʊərətitʃek] Sicherheitskontrolle
seem [si:m] scheinen, erscheinen
sense of humour [sensəv'hju:mə] Sinn für Humor
serious ['sɪəriəs] ernst
shade [ʃeɪd] Schatten
shake [ʃeɪk] schütteln
shed [ʃed]: Schuppen; Halle
shocked [ʃɒkt] schockiert
shook [ʃʊk] s.p. von **shake**
shower ['ʃaʊə]: **have a shower** duschen
signal ['sɪgnəl] Zeichen
since [sɪns] seit
sit down [sɪt'daʊn] sich setzen
six-sided [sɪks'saɪdɪd] sechsseitig
sixth-form college ['sɪksθfɔ:mkɒlɪdʒ] Oberstufenzentrum
smart [smɑ:t] schick, elegant
smell [smel] riechen
smuggle ['smʌgl] schmuggeln
solve [sɒlv] lösen
sound [saʊnd] klingen, sich anhören; **sound the horn** hupen
spite [spaɪt]: **in spite of** trotz
stare [steə] starren
start [stɑ:t] anlassen; anspringen
stick [stɪk] sich verklemmen
stick together [stɪktə'geðə] zusammenhalten
strange [streɪndʒ] seltsam
stuck [stʌk] p.p. von **stick**
stupid ['stju:pɪd] dumm
stutter ['stʌtə] stottern
such [sʌtʃ] solche/solcher/solches
suit [su:t] Anzug; Kostüm
sunglasses ['sʌnglɑ:siz] Sonnenbrille
sunset ['sʌnset] Sonnenuntergang
support [sə'pɔ:t] unterstützen
survive [sə'vaɪv] überleben
suspended sentence [sə'spendɪd'sentəns] Bewährungsstrafe
swap [swɒp] tauschen
sweat [swet] schwitzen

T

take off [teɪk'ɒf] abnehmen
tap [tæp] klopfen
tear [tɪə] Träne
test tube ['testju:b] Retorte
Thames [temz] Themse
thin [θɪn] dünn
thoughtfully ['θɔ:tfəli] nachdenklich
ticket ['tɪkɪt] Strafzettel
tie [taɪ] Schlips, Krawatte
time [taɪm] Mal; **just in time** gerade noch rechtzeitig; **on time** pünktlich
timing ['taɪmɪŋ] Timing (= Wahl des richtigen Zeitpunkts)
tough [tʌf] schwer, hart
traffic lights ['træfɪklaɪts] (Verkehrs-)Ampel
traitor ['treɪtə] Verräter/in
transport [træn'spɔ:t] transportieren, befördern
trouble ['trʌbl]: **be in trouble with** Ärger haben mit; **get into trouble** Ärger bekommen
trust [trʌst] vertrauen
truth [tru:θ] Wahrheit
try on [traɪ'ɒn] anprobieren
tube of toothpaste [tju:bəv'tu:θpeɪst] Zahnpastatube
turn around [tɜ:nə'raʊnd] sich umdrehen

U
university [ju:nɪ'vɜ:səti] Universität, Hochschule

V
vehicle ['vi:əkl] Fahrzeug
via ['vaɪə] über
view [vju:] Aussicht, Sicht
voice [vɔɪs] Stimme

W
wake up [weɪk'ʌp] aufwachen
wallet ['wɒlɪt] (Scheck-)Mäppchen
warehouse ['weəhaʊs] Lagerhalle
watch [wɒtʃ] Armbanduhr
watch out [wɒtʃ'aʊt] aufpassen
wave (to) [weɪv] (zu)winken
weak [wi:k]**: feel weak at the knees** weiche Knie bekommen
Well done! ['wel'dʌn] Gut gemacht! Bravo!
wheel [wi:l] Rad
whisper ['wɪspə] flüstern
whole [həʊl] ganz
wine [waɪn] Wein
wish [wɪʃ] wünschen
woke [wəʊk] s.p. von **wake**
wonder ['wʌndə] sich fragen
worried ['wʌrid] besorgt
worse [wɜ:s] schlechter, schlimmer
worth [wɜ:θ]**: be more than worth …** allemal … wert sein
would [wʊd] würde/würdest/ würden/würdet

Z
zip up [zɪp'ʌp] mit dem Reißverschluss schließen